For Antonia and her passion
for fairy tales and chocolate

Copyright © 2003 by Michael Neugebauer Verlag,
an imprint of Nord-Süd Verlag AG, Gossau Zürich, Switzerland
First published in Switzerland under the title Weihnachtskuchen für alle.
English translation copyright © 2003 by North-South Books Inc., New York

First published in the United States, Great Britain, Canada, Australia,
and New Zealand in 2003 by North-South Books,
an imprint of Nord-Süd Verlag AG, Gossau Zürich, Switzerland.

Distributed in the United States by North-South Books Inc., New York.

Library of Congress Cataloging-in-Publication Data is available.
A CIP catalogue record for this book is available from The British Library.
ISBN 0-7358-1885-1 (trade edition) 10 9 8 7 6 5 4 3 2 1
ISBN 0-7358-1886-X (library edition) 10 9 8 7 6 5 4 3 2 1
Printed in Italy

For more information about our books, and the authors and artists
who create them, visit our web site: www.northsouth.com

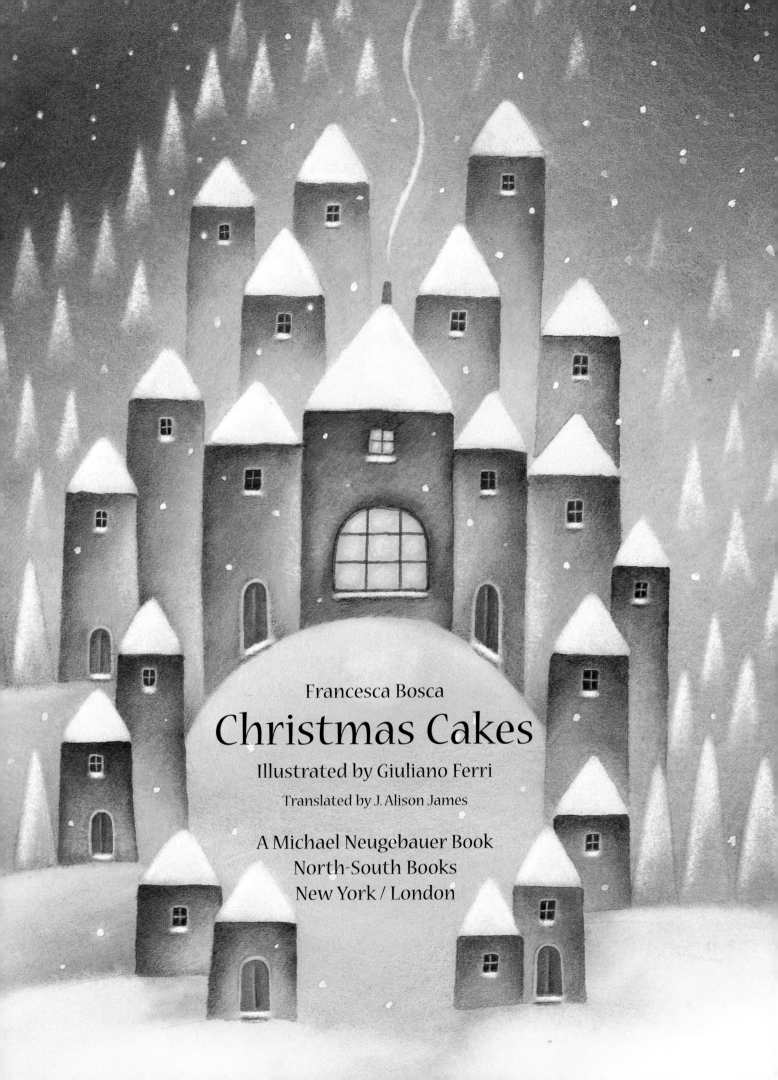

Francesca Bosca

Christmas Cakes

Illustrated by Giuliano Ferri

Translated by J. Alison James

A Michael Neugebauer Book
North-South Books
New York / London

In the bustling bakery of San Vitale, eggs were cracked, butter was creamed, and flour flew everywhere. The oven had not been turned off for days. Yet still there was much to do. Christmas was just around the corner. And Christmas would not be Christmas for the villagers in San Vitale without their precious Christmas cakes. It was a tradition.

Young Lucas helped his father in the bakery. He cracked and creamed and sifted and stirred and, after baking, he decorated every single cake with carefully chosen cherries.

At last they were finished. Aah, the heavenly scent of freshly baked Christmas cakes. They smelled of cardamom and chocolate, of falling snow and snug fires. The baker was satisfied. He and Lucas loaded up the boxes on his wagon and set off through the streets. The baker wheeled the cart while Lucas skipped along ahead and laid a package in front of every door.

But in the morning each and every cake had disappeared!

The villagers pounded on the door of the bakery
and demanded their cakes.
Lucas's father was bewildered. He had delivered
every last one, he said.
Disappointed, all the people went back home. They'd never celebrated
Christmas without a Christmas cake.

While they were talking, Lucas made a discovery.
He noticed some odd footprints in the snow.

Lucas followed the tracks from door to door. They stopped at every single house and then led out of the village. Lucas ran, following the tracks all the way to a little house right at the edge of the forest.

Lucas looked around.

He didn't see anyone.

Lucas listened.

He didn't hear anyone.

Lucas knocked. He knocked again.

Nothing.

Slowly, Lucas opened up the door and went inside.

There, piled neatly against the wall, were the missing cakes! Lucas had found them! Now what should he do? Suddenly he heard a noise. Lucas spun around. A huge and terrifying figure stood before him.

It was Otto the Woodcutter. Without a word, Otto grabbed little Lucas by the arm and locked him in a cage. Then, snarling, he sat down and began to eat.

The cakes disappeared right before Lucas's eyes. One – two – three bites and a cake was gone. Soon every cake was eaten up.

"Ooh! Aah! OW!" cried Otto the Woodcutter.

"What's wrong?" asked Lucas.

Otto held his huge stomach and rolled around in pain.

"Help! I'm going to die!"

Lucas smiled. Suddenly Otto didn't seem so dangerous after all.

"I know a cure for stomachache," he said.

"Please, please, make it for me!" moaned Otto. He freed Lucas and climbed into bed.

Lucas mixed up a bowlful of the cure, and Otto drank it all. With each sip he felt a little better.

Lucas stayed at his side. When the stomachache was all gone, Otto explained. He told about how lonely he was out in the woods, especially at Christmas. This year, he was so lonely that he grew angry. He wanted to spoil Christmas for all the happy villagers, so he decided to steal their precious Christmas cakes. "But I'm truly sorry that I did," he said sadly.

Lucas nodded, understanding. Then he jumped up. He had an idea. "Come on!" he called to Otto, and the two of them ran to the bakery.

That night, three people worked in the bakery. Lucas, his father the baker, and Otto the Woodcutter. They worked ceaselessly until dawn.

The next morning, when the villagers of San Vitale awoke, they were surprised for a second time. The air was filled with a heavenly scent and a rollicking melody danced through the streets. Curious, the villagers gathered in the middle of town .

There was a table, laden with cakes. There was the Woodcutter, playing his concertina. There was the baker with his son Lucas. And there was a cake for everyone in the village, and one more besides. This time there was a cake for Otto.

What a splendid scene! People danced and sang, ate cakes and licked cream from their fingers. Shadows grew and the sun went down, and still no one went home, such was the pleasure of celebrating Christmas together.

Lucas was the hero of the day. Otto and the others tossed him in the air, singing "Angels we have heard on High! Sweetly singing in the Sky!"

From that night on, Christmas in San Vitale had a new tradition. Christmas cake for everyone, but no one, not anyone, spent Christmas all alone!

This Is the Way to Bake a Cake:

*Chop up the chocolate
and melt it in milk*

*Beat up the eggs
Until they're like silk*

*Sift up the flour
and sugar together*

Then stir it and stir till it's
light as a feather.

Pour in a pan
and bake for an hour

Add cream and cherries
and then…devour!